International Bestselling Author

Pebbles Lacasse

ISBN 978-1-989979-69-3

This book is intended for adults only. Characters, organizations, and events portrayed are fictional. Resemblances are purely coincidental. All sexual acts are performed with persons over 21 years old.

Edited by: Off the Shelf Editing

Originally published as part of the Stuck on You charity anthology published in 2025.

TABLE OF CONTENTS

CHAPTER ONE	PAGE 5
CHAPTER TWO	PAGE 15
CHAPTER THREE	PAGE 25
CHAPTER FOUR	PAGE 37
BOOK TEASER	PAGE 53
CHAPTER ONE	PAGE 55
MORE BY PEBBLES	PAGE 77
ABOUT THE AUTHOR	PAGE 79
CONNECT WITH PEBBLES	PAGE 80
SUBSCRIBE	PAGE 81
JOIN HER TEAMS	PAGE 82
WHY DOES SHE WRITE?	PAGE 83

Dedicated to everyone who’s ever had
a secret crush.

CHAPTER ONE

It's only Wednesday, and I've already had enough of this week. As a paralegal, I'm always taking work home, and tonight will be no different. This won't be the first time I'll fall asleep among papers strewn about my bed with an empty wineglass on my nightstand.

I walk through the cubicles balancing files atop the satchel dangling from my shoulder and dread my lack of a personal life. It's been years since I had a smidgeon of a social life outside of my career. Even then it was nothing to write novels about. At twenty-six, I should be partying and enjoying life not working myself ragged.

The elevator gradually sinks from the twentieth floor with painfully annoying stops aimed to move stale-faced people from one floor to the next. Like drones, there are no smiles or greetings, just drawn faces.

The doors part for the fourth time, and my jaw clenches as I stare at the lit number ten, willing it to sail cleanly to the basement. Each shift of the elevator threatens to topple the pile of balanced files against my small breasts. My purse and overstuffed satchel weigh down my shoulder, forcing me to compensate by leaning too close to a man who could use some deodorant. At this rate, I may not make it to my car with stomach and files intact.

Maybe I should've stayed late to get this work done, but it's never ending whether I remain go home. I could just say fuck it and stop working at five o'clock like most of my coworkers, but it's not who I am. Call me compulsive, but once I start something I have to see its completion.

The silver doors slide open with a quiet female voice announcing that we've arrived on the seventh floor. Two overly chatty people exit leaving me alone, which could mean a smooth sail to the basement.

Just as the doors are about to close, an arm dressed in a navy-blue suit jacket juts through the slot and the doors retreat.

Dammit!

I'm about to growl under my breath when my attractive boss's boss strolls in as if he has all the time in the world. I suppose being the CEO of a Fortune 500 corporation means handing down tasks one prefers not to perform, thus allotting plenty of time to lazily stroll about.

Good for him, but others—like myself—don't wish to doddle. Sure, I've fantasized about bouncing on him like a pogo stick, but elevator quickies stem from writers. They aren't reality.

A blend of leather and musk cologne seduces my nostrils, and I can't help but breathe him in.

The 6'4" man commands every room he enters, including this tiny tin box. His shoulders square to the closing doors before he notices me off to his right. It's subtle, but his eyelids narrow as they drink in my white silk blouse, burgundy pin skirt, and matching suit jacket. I'm well-aware my skirt and blouse bear the wrinkles of a long day sat in an office chair, but I'm too burnt out to care.

Mr. Grant has been the source of many erotic dreams, and they're exhausting. Because of him I have tiny purple pillows taking up residence beneath my eyes, and I drag a virtual saggy, weighted ass along the floor with each step despite my tiny frame. But the memories of those dreams make it all worthwhile.

The sexy man is often the topic of discussions near the watercooler because he's perfection in a well-fitted suit: tall and thick like a gym rat, with short black hair styled as if a professional follows him around with a comb at the ready.

The few times we've met eyes, I had to look away. If I had stared too long into his black orbs, would he peer into my soul and hear my thoughts?

He watches me fuss to dig my phone from my purse to start my car remotely. The winter's bone-chilling temperatures are something I'd rather avoid.

His hands ease into the pockets of his dress pants as his chin lifts ever so slightly. His voice is low and husky. "Hello, Lauren."

A thousand people work in the building, and he knows my name?

"Hello, Mr. Gra—" My case load slides from my arm just as I yank my phone free. In trying to grab the folders, I fling my phone against the mirrored elevator wall. A loud crack proves either my phone or the mirrored wall broke, maybe both. But the paperwork ends up strewn across the elevator floor, halting against his shiny black shoe.

Oh, my God! Way to make a good impression on your boss's boss, Lauren!

My purse and satchel slide off my arm and hit the floor when I drop to my knees. As quickly as possible, I reach for each manilla folder and tuck papers back inside them. Damn my decision to carry them loosely against my chest. I look like a jackass on my knees in front of my sinfully handsome boss.

With a voice so deep my body rattles, he says, "Let me help you."

He crouches in front of me, stacks three folders on his palm, and lifts them toward me. We're so near a potent waft of his masculine cologne dances through my senses. My nostrils defy me by snorting in a deep breath as if I'm an addict and he is my vice. Is it the cologne or our approximation that has my head spinning?

I cough hoping to mask an unintentional whimper that rides my exhale.

My pussy clenches, reminding me she's sexually frustrated. But this man carries himself all business. He'd have no interest in someone beneath his station, like me. So, don't make a fool of yourself by flirting!

How long has it been since I had a man between my legs? Three years? Not since Reggie split, leaving me with two months back rent, an empty bank account, and a mountain of debt. Fucking Reggie!

His sharp tone annunciates every word. "Why do you have so many files? Are you a company spy?"

I wince as all the blood drains from my face. "What? No! I—I'm not a spy. This is—I didn't finish, so I—I have to take things home to—"

Oh, my God! Stop talking you babbling buffoon!

With a disarming crooked grin, he whispers, "That was a joke."

Blood creeps up to flood my cheeks. My face dips to hide my embarrassment as I slip my phone into my purse and sigh with relief it isn't. broken. Thankfully, the mirror is intact as well.

I set the pile of folders he rescued on top of the ones balancing on my forearm and pin them to my chest before I nod and twitch my lips into a smile.

My stare follows his smooth movements as he rises to stand tall.

His groin is so close to my face it'd be easy to unzip his pants to release what hides behind the bulge of grey fabric and live out a fantasy that's haunted so many of my dreams.

The bulge bewilders me: Is he aroused or very well-endowed? Just how big is that thing?

Stop fucking looking!

My lashes flutter as I hug the files tighter to my breast. "I'm not a spy. I try to keep up to the workload, but there's always more to do, and I'm only one person." My breathy laugh stops me from complaining about how my boss is a hard-ass who overloads me.

Thick fingers extend from a sizeable palm down to me when I shuffle on my knees to maintain my balance.

"Let me carry your files." He insists, but I shake my head.

"No, no. I have them."

Disregarding my stubbornness, the gentleman in him grips under my bicep and lifts me effortlessly to my feet. Fully upright, the top of my head is level with his shoulder. He releases me, and I tug to move the straps to my purse and satchel to stop them from digging my bra strap deeper into my shoulder.

My face tilts away shyly as I tuck a stray lock of auburn hair behind my ear. "Thank you."

His reputation as a man of few words proves invalid as his smooth as silk baritone voice demands my attention. "You work on the twentieth floor, right?"

He visits our floor almost daily but rushes past the cubicles on his way to meetings in the conference room or my boss's office. It's rare to not see him face down in his phone as he strides past us.

"You know where I work?" I grimace when I notice him gazing down at my cleavage. Awkward!

He takes a slow, deep breath as his hands imprison themselves in his pants pockets. "You're always so deep into your work you rarely look up to see who's watching you."

Watching me?

The air grows hellishly hot when his tongue pokes free to moisten his lips. My chest to my face ignites in flames—at least, that's what it feels like.

What I wouldn't give to have those full, masculine lips encircling my clitoris while his tongue teases and caresses beneath its hood.

For the love of God, Lauren!

"I j—just work a lot. My job is demanding and—and sometimes it's—a lot." I take a step back and level my face to his chest. Why do I feel like a high school nerd cornered by the quarterback?

I stiffen when Mr. Grant closes the space between us. His forefinger brushes along my cheek as it captures that same stubborn lock of hair and tenderly tucks it behind my ear. The heat from his finger, despite not having touched my skin, radiates directly to my nipples.

His voice hums in a sedate whisper as I drown in his mesmerizing stare. “If you can pull yourself away from your desk tomorrow, come up to my office.”

Still under his spell, my voice is weak. “Go up to— Why?”

His whisper is gruff as his face tilts lower to mine. “Why not? I’d like to get to know you better, Lauren.”

Well, knock me over with a light wind! A strangled laugh escapes me.

His chuckle is muted as his brows creep up toward the lines etched into his forehead. “I will never lie to you, Lauren.”

A finger lifts my chin to force my jerky gaze to still on his hypnotizing ebony orbs. His deep voice vibrates like a seductive invitation. “You’ll come to my office at eleven-thirty. There’s something I’d like to discuss with you. I’ll arrange lunch for us.”

“Lunch—” My heart thrums noisily in my ears as I nod without thinking. Snap out of it! “Um, okay. Well, my lunch doesn’t start until noon, but I can see if Ms. Granger will—”

Mr. Grant remains dangerously close to me. “Don’t worry about a thing. She’ll be informed. She may be a tough boss but she always gets the job done.”

All I can do is nod, but my overworked inner voice is pissed that he thinks she's the one working hard when it's *me* she saddles with hours of work at home every night.

Wait… Why aren't we descending?

Panic!

My attention freezes on the flashing panel of numbers as my finger pounds the button for the basement floor, but the numbers continue to blink. My heart begins to race as I continually poke the button while gaping at the glowing number seven above the closed metal doors.

Is the air in here getting thinner? Oh God! I can't breathe.

"Did you just realise we aren't moving?" How is he still so dignified when the air is being squeezed out of this tiny box as it shrinks around us?

"I don't like elevators. Confined spaces— I can't—" My hand clutches my chest to ease the panic attack threatening to mortify me in front of the CEO.

Strong hands rest atop my shoulders and give me a little shake to direct my attention on him. Minty breath and masculine cologne tease my nostrils. "We're okay. It's only a glitch. It won't last long."

My head shakes wildly as my tingling tear ducts threaten to dump a truckload of waterworks down my bloodless cheeks.

Do not cry in front of the big boss-man!

His hushed tone is stern but nonthreatening. “Lauren, take a deep breath.”

He takes the files from my arm with the cautiousness of a man taking food from a lion. He sets them on the floor in a neat stack, along with my purse and satchel, before his eyes bore into mine.

He draws so near that his lips hover just above mine.

Elevator? What elevator?

“Lauren—”

CHAPTER TWO

His thick tongue glides over his bottom lip, stealing a whimper from me.

"Mr. Grant, I, um. I'm—" I inhale too quickly and my head spins.

He stares fiercely into my soul as he whispers so seductively, it should be a sin. "Tell me not to kiss you."

This has got to be a dream. My toes wiggle to ensure I'm wearing shoes; I'm always barefoot in my dreams. Holy, shit!

Is this really happening!?

Thick fingers brush around my neck to the back of my head and fist into my hair. It hurts as he gradually tips my head back to allow his lips to graze from my clavicle to my jaw, where he nips with his teeth.

Well, set me on fire! I want to reach out to touch him, but my arms remain ramrod stiff at my sides.

Puffy lips brush my cheek at the edge of my mouth, but he doesn't kiss me. "Tell me to stop, Lauren."

I shiver as if lost in an ice storm when I should melt from the heat of this scalding man standing before me. My lungs no longer restrain my voice. “Don’t stop.”

Not a second passes before fervent lips crush mine, and his tongue forces its way inside to dance over my teeth.

This can’t be happening! Arron Grant has been the focus of my masturbatory material for years, and now it’s coming to fruition? In an elevator?! If those doors open, our coworkers will see us. They’ll report us to HR. I’ll likely lose my job while he gets pats on his back by his peers.

I reach up and press my palms to his chest. In the time it takes to blink, he clutches my wrists in one hand and holds them behind my back. The powerful man nearly lifts me as he presses me firmly against the icy elevator wall.

He breathes slow and deep as his forehead rests against mine. His free hand eases down my waist to my hip. My skirt rises higher up my legs as he gathers the material in his fist.

“Tell me to stop, Lauren. Tell me to stop or I won’t.”

“Mr. Grant—” My breath catches when fingers brush over my cotton panties covering my mound. The jolt of electricity weakens my knees. He braces his knee against my leg to keep it from buckling.

"Tell me to stop, Lauren." A finger presses firmly over my panties between my labia and my hips buck forward instinctively.

I don't recognize my voice channeling a sex-starved character in a romance novel. "Don't stop."

His tongue invades my mouth as he yanks my panties down my thighs to my knees. A long, strong finger feeds between my labia down to my slick vagina. My walls spread as the digit eases inside. Is the elevator spinning like a washing machine?

This can't be happening. I'll wake in my bed at any moment—shoes be damned.

My moan fills his mouth as his finger glides up to lubricate my clitoris with my arousal. Gentle swirls over the stiffening nub drop my head back against the elevator wall. His lips leave mine to travel down my chin to the cleft of my throat.

Before I can stop him, he grips the fabric of my blouse and yanks until all the buttons rip free. I yelp as tiny plastic buttons ricochet off the walls and onto the floor. He grips my bra and jerks it, bouncing my breasts free. The motion steals my breath, but my back instinctually arches my breasts toward his mouth.

His tongue encircles my right nipple, teasing it into submission. Bolts of lightning shoot to my clit, edging me closer to climax.

My words whimper with pathetic urgency. "Oh, God. Please. Mr. Grant, please."

A finger eases between my labia until it slips into my vagina. My breath catches when he thrusts in before pulling out, only to add a second digit. They delve deep and spread like scissors to stretch my walls.

Delicious pain ripples through my chest when his teeth latch onto my nipple. More a scream, my moan echoes off the metal walls.

He releases my wrists to cover my mouth. His leer burns lustfully into mine as he threatens me. "Not a sound. Do you understand?"

There's no way to speak with his hand against my mouth. Nodding is impossible with my head pressed firmly against the elevator wall.

I grip onto his dress shirt with all of my strength to keep him doing what he's doing.

His eyes never leave mine as his fingers glide out of my vagina and pinch my clitoris. Alternating strokes, the digits brush the hood of my clitoris back and forth across my most sensitive bundle of nerves.

No man has ever gotten this move right. Yet here is my boss's boss—a man of great wealth and power—teasing my femininity into submission. At this moment, I'd do anything he asked if only he continued this sensational torture.

He whispers against his hand covering my mouth as if trying to kiss me through it. "Do you want to cum, Lauren?"

My plea escapes my nostrils, and my lids pinch closed to prevent him from devouring my soul.

"Eyes on me," he growls.

With reservation, I comply.

"Good girl."

I should detest his belittling yet praising words—*good girl*—but I don't.

His hand leaves my mouth but grips my throat and presses on either side of my esophagus. Tiny stars soon dance over my vision. Pressure builds inside my belly with each brush of his fingers around my clitoris.

"Open your eyes, Lauren. I want you to see who's stealing your orgasm."

I hadn't realized they'd closed. My lids flutter open to see a fire blaze in his face.

The heat from his fingers sends an electrical current straight up to my belly button where a balloon has swollen inside me. The larger it grows, the greater the tickle until it's too much to restrain.

My entire being teeters on the edge of blissful death, and I want nothing more than to give into it.

Flashes dance in my vision and increase until the bright white of their cluster blinds me with light so intense I'm sure I'm dying.

The tickles erupt from my clitoris outward, overtaking my being. I float in the most glorious pleasure while my fists clutch his dress shirt to keep from floating away.

Clarity rushes back as the stars clear. A gasp fills my lungs, but my orgasm continues to pummel me like an ocean's surf. My body stiffens and jerks as my ragged breaths come in short bursts.

His slitted eyes bore into mine, urging another much stronger wave of pleasure to sweep away my sanity.

His mouth covers mine to capture my scream. My death grip on his crisp shirt keeps me upright despite my boneless legs.

The instant his fingers withdraw, my swollen, hypersensitive pussy is lonely. His stare holds mine as his fingers sink into his mouth and he moans appreciatively.

Swoon!

His blink lingers as he suckles the digits. He moans as if my flavour is better than any dessert he's savoured.

They glisten as they ease from his lips. Crow's feet deepen the outer edges of his eyes as his crooked smile lifts his puffy lips.

How does this man remain so collected while I'm a disheveled mess?

Mr. Grant steps back, bends forward, and helps me step out of my panties. I really wish I'd worn prettier lingerie today, but never could I have predicted this elevator adventure.

His eyelids flutter as he presses the material to his nose and breathes them in before sliding them into the inside pocket of his suit coat. "These are mine now."

I have neither the strength nor desire to argue with him. Besides, he's earned them.

Should I return the favour? My shaky hand reaches for his belt, but his palm covers mine.

He winks just before he kisses my cheek. "Not now."

"But you must need to—"

"My needs can wait. Touching you was enough to satisfy me for the moment. Do you have any idea how long I've desired to watch you cum: to see your eyes roll back and know it's my touch that granted so much pleasure?"

His thick index finger lifts my chin as he looks down his perfectly straight nose. "I expect you in my office tomorrow at 11:30. Are we clear?"

I try to swallow the cotton ball in my throat and fail. "Yes, sir."

The palm of his hand strokes the top of my head like one would a favoured pet. This should mortify me, but the way he tips his head awakens my shy smile.

What the fuck is happening to me?

Seriously, all it takes is one earth-shattering orgasm to turn me into a mushy puddle? I'm a strong, independent woman who needs no approval from a man. Yet, here I am, blushing before this powerful male specimen as he pets my head. I'd do anything for him.

I wiggle my breasts back into my bra and pull my jacket closed to fasten the buttons to conceal my torn blouse. Hopefully, nobody will notice.

Mr. Grant collects the stacked files, my purse, and satchel from the floor and hands them to me, making sure they're secure in my grip. His shoes scuff the elevator floor as he crosses the small silver box and slips a key into the slot below the flashing numbers. He turns it to the right and presses a button to shut off the flashing numbers. He removes the key, stuffs it in his pocket, and smirks at me as he pushes the button bearing the number five.

"Wait… *You* stopped the elevator?"

His brows creep up on his forehead, proving he did.

"When? I didn't see you do anything."

"You were distracted by the files on the floor, so I took advantage. Sorry to frighten you, but wasn't that fun?"

I'd fallen for his smooth, deceitful intensions. I'd believed he was my saviour; the one to comfort me when panic nearly stole my sanity. I'd fallen into his arms like a sex-starved floozy—just as he'd intended. He'd twisted me into believing he was genuine.

"I'm such an idiot." I turn my body from him to rest my shoulder against the wall and glare straight ahead. "How many women have you done this with?"

"Lauren, I've never done—" His words cut off as the doors open to an awaiting crowd.

Three people wearing frustration on their pursed lips stroll in. A woman scrutinizes me before shifting her attention to Mr. Grant. She gazes back at my rosy cheeks as her brows rise and her lips twist knowingly. More than anything, I want to slap the 'I know what you did, and I'm going to tell everyone' expression off her snobby face.

To explain my dishevelled appearance, I raise my voice as he steps out of the elevator. "Sorry I panicked when the elevator got stuck."

Taking my cue without a second to spare, he replies, "I'm glad I could help."

The doors close as an elderly man glances at me with a sympathetic nod. The woman scoffs, and I imagine cracking the back of her head with my files so hard her face meets the metal elevator doors. She looks like the type to spread rumors around the watercooler—a nosy Nancy with a jealous chip on her shoulder. Bitch!

Finally, I lock myself in my car. If I were still wearing panties, I could deny what had actually happened, but the slickness between my labia and the cool air blowing up my skirt from the unheated air vent prove otherwise.

Purposeful or not, that ride was sexy as hell.

My boss's boss masturbated me in an office elevator, and now he wants me in his office. Oh, how I wish it were tomorrow!

CHAPTER THREE

Through bloodshot eyes that haven't rested, I watch the sun rise. Haunting concerns about what may happen in Mr. Grant's office has made my sleep fitful.

What will he do with me today, if anything? Has the time between then and now made him to understand that what we did goes against all the HR rules? Will he apologize for his actions with a promise to never touch me inappropriately again?

I don't want that. I should, but I don't.

The fact is, he's my boss—more than that, he's the CEO. If we were to become a couple, nine years of hard work and endless late nights at the office will become irrelevant. Any promotion I get from here on will be seen as earned on my back, no matter the effort my coworkers see me putting into my job.

I scoff into my third mug of coffee. I'm a fucking idiot to think a man of his station would want a relationship with a nobody like me. He wants sex, nothing more. I'd be a fool to dream otherwise.

I should march into his top floor office and set him straight. This can't happen again!

I should, but my body begs the opposite.

"Fucking hell!"

***

Two hours into my workday and nobody's looked at me sideways. Maybe I misjudged the woman in the elevator.

Time passes too quickly. My indecisiveness has me chewing my cheek until I taste copper. Should I go to him as he requested or leave the building to eat at the diner across the street?

A memo pops up on my computer's screen. Ms. Granger wants to see me in her office.

I knock twice before her shrill voice calls out, "Come in."

Her office smells of new carpet and misery.

"You want to see me?" I sit in one of the dark blue fabric chairs opposite her disorganized oak desk.

"Yes." She closes her laptop before leaning back in her chair to assess my cleavage escaping my low-cut dress. "Mr. Grant has requested to see you in his office at 11:30. I don't know why. Do you?"

Yes. He wants to ravish me sexually in the privacy of his office.

"No. Though he helped me through a panic attack when the elevator got stuck yesterday." Well, that's not a lie. "Maybe he wants to check on me?"

"Hmm." Her stubby fingers form a peak below her nose as she studies me with scrutinizing blue eyes shrouded by bushy brows that could benefit from a wax. "I haven't put in for a promotion on your behalf, so it's not that."

Of course she won't promote me. She'd lose her best worker.

My shoulders lift as my lids widen. "I suppose he'll let me know when I get there."

"Mmm, yes. I suppose he will." She rocks forward on her chair, whips open her laptop, and shoos me away with a wave of her hand. "Take your lunch after he's finished with you. We have a lot of work to do this afternoon."

We?

"I will." As if my ass is on fire, I rush from her office to my cubicle.

I take my purse from beneath my desk and make my way to the washroom to primp and pee.

Succumb to his will or not, I don't plan to make this easy on him. I want him to know I feel sexy today. My choice for slightly higher heels was purposeful to slim my legs. My deep red, form-fitting dress stops just above my knees.

My lingerie match today. They're lacy and the same shade as my dress. No boring white cotton panties. Nope. If he's going to steal my undies, they're going to be pretty and feminine. If he does, my bra will no longer have a match, but I don't wear the set often enough to care.

Did he lie in his bed in the dark with my panties held to his nose while he fisted his cock? Did he stroke himself to my scent until his muscles tightened, face contorted, and he wailed my name as he shot his load on his perfectly formed Adonis belt?

I stuff my brush back in my purse as my cherry cheeked reflection stares back at me with lustful intentions. "Get it together."

Every step to his office requires concentration. One lapse and my knees may give out, toppling me to the floor.

Just breathe. It'll be okay.

He may innocently want to have lunch to talk, nothing more. Inviting me to eat with him could stem from honourable intentions. It's possible, right?

Stepping out of the elevator, there's no sound as my heels meet the pale grey carpet that spans the entire common area. The lower portion of the walls are burgundy, while the top is pale grey to match the carpet. Every photo hung with precision shows nature at its finest, with vast expanses of forestry, rock faces, waterfalls, and pools of blue I could see myself swimming naked in.

Mr. Grant's office is at the end of the short hall lined with floor to wall windows.

Stopping a foot before his closed heavy wooden door, my hands shake, so I squeeze them into fists and take a deep breath. Before I can knock, a hand on my back startles me.

The woman is tall and thin. Her long, silky blonde hair and immaculately applied make-up has her looking like a rich snob. "You must be Ms. Greyson. He's expecting you."

"Please, call me Lauren."

She returns my smile. "I'm Martina Marris. It's lovely to meet you."

"It's nice to meet you, t—"

"You can go right in." Her palm raises toward the placard on the door.

"Thank you." My shaking fingers grip the door handle.

Martina smiles before she walks off with her clutch under her arm. Her three-inch heels make no sound as her perfectly sculpted ass sways below a tiny waist.

Was she cut from a catalogue? She's got a body a Victoria's Secret model would envy. If he has her to look at all day, why choose me? Do I look desperate?

Who am I kidding? I *am* desperate.

My knuckles rap on the solid oak door before I open it.

"Ms. Greyson, please come in." Mr. Grant stands from his black leather office chair and buttons his suit coat without thought, as if he's done it a million times.

The door closes behind me with a hushed click that startles me. A hint of leather and musk lingers in the cool air. Something else seduces my nostrils—Thai food?

Despite the entire wall of floor to ceiling windows, the room is dim with soft lighting. A black leather sofa sits in the middle of the room facing a shiny grey table. Opposite are two matching sofa chairs that look like they could swallow a person in their softness.

More paintings of nature grab my attention as they hover with perfect alignment. I'm envious because every photo hung at home is crooked. No matter how often I level them, the next day they'll be off kilter.

Everything in this office is in perfect order. Even his oversized, wood desk with its raw edges shines with perfection, everything in its place. Is he always so precise, or did he tidy up for my benefit?

His smile is slight as a hand on my lower back leads me toward his desk. After he seats me in one of the high-backed leather chairs, I watch him round the desk and ease himself onto his chair.

Seconds tick by and the silence has my ears ringing.

Much to my surprise, my voice is steady. "Why am I here?"

His elbows rest on the hardwood surface as he leans forward, his index finger brushing his bottom lip—the lip that melted against mine not twenty hours ago.

"Ms. Greyson, I have a proposition for you. It's extremely inappropriate for the office, but here we are." Is there a hint of tension in his tone?

"Okay. How inappropriate?" My fingers lace together in my lap as I cross one thigh over the other while his eyes follow the motion. Why do I sense a shift in power, as if I'm in control?

He clears his throat and cradles his chin in his hand. "Yesterday was just a small part of what I have planned for us."

What the fuck? There's more?!

"Wow! We are just jumping right in here." My fingers tuck my locks behind my ear as I shuffle on the chair. "Okay. Please elaborate."

His throat clears as he pulls several sheets of paper from a drawer and slides them toward me. Leaning forward, the words *Legal Contract* draw my attention.

"What's this?" I try to make sense of it, but only certain words jump out at me: Submissive. Dominant. Bondage. Sex. Dungeon.

Noting my hesitation, his voice softens. "Don't be put off. This is a contract between us I am asking you to sign. It states that we're entering a dominant/submissive relationship and that neither of us can tell anyone anything that happens between us."

My palm pats the papers as the other presses onto my thigh. “So, it’s an NDA. I already signed an NDA when I started at this company.”

Mr. Grant leans forward and continues to speak slowly, as if worried he’ll frighten me. “This non-disclosure agreement is much more personal. Lauren, I’d like to take you on a journey of self-discovery. Whether you admit it or not, you’re a submissive, and I want you to be mine.”

My palms rub over my thighs as a strangled sounding laugh rings too loud. “How can you assume that I’m a submissive? You don’t know me. I am not in need of instruction nor am I a pathetic push over.”

As a peace offering, his palm stretches toward me. “Lauren, a submissive isn’t pathetic or a push over. You misunderstand the word. A submissive holds all the power in a D/s relationship.”

I scoff and swallow hard as my hand swings between us. “Um, no. The sub isn’t the one holding the damn whip and bludgeoning herself.”

His chuckle masks the barest trace of a smirk. “That’s true in most cases. But it’s the sub that permits the dominant’s actions.”

“Bullshit!” My back straightens as my arms hug my chest.

His chin rises as he wears the semblance of a frown. “Don’t shut down.”

My fingernails scrape my head. “Shut down?”

"When you first sat down, you crossed your legs and placed your hands together on your thighs tucked in close to your body. That told me you were nervous and a little aroused, but trying to remain proper. Right now, your leg is swinging under the desk, your back is stiff, and your lips tight. You're pushing me away."

"So, you're an insightful dominant. Outstanding. Tell me what I'm thinking now."

His tongue pokes free to taste his bottom lip. He leans back in his chair and rests his forearms on the armrests. With a slight tilt of his head, a slow breath eases from him. "You want to say yes because you're curious, but by doing so, you don't want me to think of you as weak."

Holy fuck! He can read my thoughts.

He continues, "You watched my tongue wet my lips which proved you find me sexually attractive. When I leaned back, your eyes fell to my chest and you swallowed. You looked at my right hand for a solid three seconds—the hand that brought you pleasure in the elevator. But then you lifted your chin and held my gaze."

This man can read me like an open book, and that book is erotica. I'm in so much trouble.

His voice softens as he leans in. "How about we eat, and you can ask me all the questions you have bouncing around in that pretty little head of yours."

"I don't think I can eat right now. My stomach is—"

"Nervous. That's understandable." He stands and rounds his desk with the kind of smooth sophistication only proper etiquette teaches. His stare demands my attention as he slowly turns my chair to face him and lowers to one knee before me. Nothing about his expression shows malice or ill intent. "What would you like me to clarify about my proposal?"

My ramble is quick as I look everywhere but at him. "What do you want from me? How will this affect my career if we're found out? Do you want me to live with you on weekends like that movie with Mr. Grey? Is this a relationship or simply a physical thing? Are you going to hurt me? I just don't know—" The threat of tears burn behind my lids, but a deep breath wards them away.

I can't look up from the thick hands spanned across my thighs. Their comforting warmth burns deep into my skin. My entire body heats more the longer he touches me.

"I don't expect you to stay with me unless that's your choice. Pain is also your choice. You decide how far to take it, and I get the final say in whether it's appropriate for you. All Dom/sub commitments are a relationship, at least on some level." His hands give my thighs a squeeze to redirect my eyes to his. "We can see how well we mesh and define our relationship from there. If you only want physical confrontation, we'll avoid any interaction construed as romantic, but I hope that's not the case."

He takes my hands in his so his thumbs brush the backs. The cold from the absence of his heated palms on my thighs has me considering his proposal simply to escape my mundane existence. He promises to introduce me to a lifestyle I know nothing about—a way to add some fire in my lethargic love life. And yet, the threat of greater disappointment sobers me.

My voice cracks. "And my career?"

"Your career is not under threat and never will be. You're a hard worker with too heavy of a workload, and I'd never stand in the way of your goals. I promise never to promote you to a higher position without merit, and guarantee your standing won't fall if this doesn't work out between us. I'd hate to lose such an exceptional employee." Kindness and understanding radiate from Mr. Grant's ebony eyes.

"What the hell. Okay. But first, you have to tell me what to do. I mean, I don't need a step-by-step guide, but if you make me feel like a fucking idiot because I'm naïve to the Dom/sub thing, I'll walk away faster than you can beg me not to."

He smiles as if I've just offered him a free pony. "That's fair."

I take a deep breath and let my shoulders drop. "So, where do we start? I mean, you brought me to your office during lunch hour to ensure your assistant is nowhere to be seen for a reason, right?" My teeth clutch my upper lip to repress a nervous smile.

"Yes." His Adam's apple bobs. He stands and offers his palm to me.

My hand slips into his, and I stand with my head tilted back to look up at him.

"I desire to bind your arms behind your back, bend you over my desk, and hold you at the edge of orgasm until you beg me to let you cum." He kisses my knuckles as his eyes are veiled in shadows. "Say yes."

How the fuck can any hot-blooded woman say no to that? That's the juiciest proposal I've ever gotten.

"Yes."

CHAPTER FOUR

Mr. Grant presses a kiss to my forehead as his arms wrap around my shoulders to ease the zipper down my back. The whoosh of the tines separating sounds like a jackhammer in the silent room.

His fingertips brush down my bare back as he squats low enough to grip the hem of my dress and lift it over my head. As it leaves my arms, my hair falls to my shoulders. A chill licks at my skin but cannot cool the fire smouldering beneath.

I stand before him in my red lace thong, matching bra, and high heels. No matter how much I tell myself to breathe, every breath sticks in my throat.

He rests the dress on the side of the desktop and stands before me. His nearness is reassuring, but not enough to slow my racing heart. I can't look up from the white button on his dress shirt that is level with my eyes.

"You shake from adrenaline. It's normal in this situation." He watches his fingertips as they ease down my temple, cheek, and along my neck to my nape. "Stay here."

He needn't tell me that; my muscles have gone rigid. If I were to walk, I'd likely fall on my face or stumble as taut as Frankenstein. Sexy!

In seconds, he's behind me. The heat of his breath warms my left shoulder before he places a kiss on it. "You are so beautiful. Never forget how you drive me wild."

I drive him wild? Flattery will get you everything, Arron Grant.

He guides my hand behind me until my palm cups his raging hard cock. It fills my hand and then some. Gasp! He's thick, at least, he feels thick shrouded beneath the fabric of his tailored dress pants.

A tender kiss presses to the top of my head before he steps back and glides rope along my spine. His tone seems too composed for the pending act. "I'm going to bind your arms behind your back. If it's too much and you want me to stop, I'll cut you free in a matter of seconds. All you have to say is *Red*. Red stops the scene immediately. Do you understand?"

The delicate cotton rope brushes across my lower back over the waistband of my panties, urging fear and something else; desire, curiosity perhaps.

Parched, my words fall shy. "What if I'm—what if I just need a minute?"

He rounds me and lifts my chin with one finger. "Eyes on me." His black orbs ooze compassion dripping with salacious desire. "If you need to pause the scene, say *Yellow*. I'll pause to ask if you want to stop or continue."

So, I do have a say in what happens. Maybe when he said that the submissive holds the power, he was telling the truth.

"Do you trust me?" His fingertips glide over my neck. Ripples of shivers like a stone skipped on a calm lake weaken my resolve.

"I suppose I have no choice at this point but to trust you." My nervous chuckle has me internally rolling my eyes. This is not the time to laugh!

He guides my arms to cross over my back until my hands grip either forearm. The rope encircles both multiple times, cinching my forearms together, thus forbidding movement.

This is it. Arron Grant is going to take control over me and, strangely enough, I'm thrilled to be the physical object of his entertainment: to do whatever he requests of me.

His unquivering breath precedes his low whisper. "I promise to earn your trust."

The ends of the rope no longer tickle my buttocks as he manipulates it. His hands leave me, and my shoulders pull forward to test the limitation of my movements.

I'd never considered bondage as something that would thrill me, but here I am with a damp pussy, panting from excitement.

The man's silence should have me freaking out, but the anticipation of his touch is more thrilling than any amusement ride. Should I turn to look at him or does he prefer to admire his work undisturbed?

The heat from his words singe the air. "Fuck, Lauren. You are perfection. I'm honoured you trust me enough to offer yourself to me in this way. Will you allow me to fuck you?"

The room falls into darkness as his silken lips graze my neck from behind.

Oh my God, this man is going to be the death of me!

My whisper quivers. "Do you have a condom?"

My eyelids open when the familiar rattle of a condom rapper in my face is proof he respects me enough to offer peace of mind. He thought ahead; I didn't.

This is really happening. My smoulderingly sexy boss's boss is going to fuck me on his desk in his office where anyone could walk in. The door isn't locked and we are within business hours. Even if his assistant is on her lunch break, the rest of the office workers are humming about. Anyone could hear us.

Why does the excitement of getting caught have me giddy like a goddamn psychopath?! Stop smiling!

With his hands on my shoulders, he guides me to the back of his desk and kicks his chair out of the way. "Spread your legs, bend forward, and place your cheek on the desk."

My bottom lip pinches between my teeth so hard I fear the skin may puncture, but I do as he orders. The wood is cool against my nearly nude body, but I barely feel it.

Hot palms glide down my waist, leaving tiny prickles in their wake. Fingers loop under the waistband of my panties and ease them down my legs with incredible patience. He lifts each foot to remove them. I hear him breathe in deeply, and picture how his blink lingered when he inhaled the scent of my panties yesterday.

An unexpected hot, fat, wet tongue laps from my clit to my asshole as his hands squeeze my ass cheeks to pull them apart. My back arches as my guttural wail fades into the walls.

Oh. My. God!

My arms struggle against their binding. The more I fight against the rope, the more the threat excites me.

Is it the rope or the forfeit of control that is my kink?

Soft lips encircle my swelling clitoris and suck as his tongue manipulates the tiny bud. Every nerve in my body is on fire.

His hands grip the creases at the bottom edge of my butt cheeks as his thumbs spread my labia, offering him full access to my throbbing clit. The way his tongue seems to vibrate every sensitive feminine nerve has me teetering on the edge of orgasm in seconds. No man has gotten me here so quickly. Even masturbation takes longer than this.

"Beg me to cum, Lauren." His words pull me back from falling into my pleasure.

"Please. Please let me cum." My voice sounds distant.

"Be a good girl and call me sir."

I'll call him Mr. President if it pleases him. "Sir, please. Please let me cum, sir."

"You're such a good girl."

His pinky and index fingers hold my labia apart as the center two dive deep into my vagina. The room spins. I buck against his digits as my clit pulses from the absence of his tongue.

My face lifts from the desktop as a foreign, guttural moan carries a plea that fills the room. "Sir, please!"

His fingers vacate. I'm about to cry out when he instructs,. "Open your mouth."

Before I can ask why, he shoves my panties inside.

Low, deep, and carnal, he whispers, "Make a sound, and I won't let you cum." Mr. Greyson taps my hand so I'll open my fist, and places three pens into my palm. "If you need me to stop for any reason, drop the pens. Nod your head if you understand."

Unable to speak, I nod my understanding and rest my forehead on the desktop.

Fingers plunge back into me while he laps and sucks on my clitoris. The two digits bump something solid toward the front of my vagina. Each thump sends a shockwave to my clit, and it's the sweetest torture.

If he doesn't let me cum, I'll surely die a gruesome death—implosion, perhaps, or mental insanity.

He told me to ask to cum, but also wants me silent. My muffled mumbles aren't decipherable as language, but he seems to understand.

"Cum, pretty Lauren. Cum for me."

That's all I need to let go. My body and mind float higher with each flutter of his tongue and thump from his fingers. An unexpected brush of his finger over my anus has me spiraling over the edge into pure exultation. I float weightlessly among the shadows of nothingness. I'm free and it's pure ecstasy.

Mr. Grant's fingers and tongue pet my soul as I offer it to him. Take me. I'm yours.

Restriction around my throat crashes me back to reality. A hand eases my upper body off the desk while restricting my breathing. I'd be afraid—if that orgasm hadn't left me so elated that even the threat of death doesn't frighten me.

He removes the panties from my mouth before his hand settles on my jaw, and turns my chin to see his intense, predatory glare.

My arms are sore from pulling, but I like the pain and restriction. He has me in his clutches and it's exactly where I want to be.

Growly and needy, his words singe my ear. "I'm going to fuck you so goddamn hard you'll beg me to cum. Tell me to stop, Lauren."

Why does he want me to tell him to stop if he so desperately wants to fuck me?

I try to whisper, "No," but the dryness of my throat makes me hoarse.

His steely shaft presses between my ass cheeks. Holy hell, how thick is it?

Sharp teeth nip my earlobe before his rumbly voice grows more insistent. "Tell me to stop and I will."

"Fuck me!" I beg, gasping the moment his teeth sink into my shoulder. "Fuck me hard. Please, sir, I need you inside me."

Who is this desperate woman with the potty mouth? This can't be me. Am I that good girl turned slut in erotic novels—the one who gets the best fucking of her life? God, I hope so.

Goosebumps pepper my skin as his fingertips coast down my spine. His voice is gravelly. "Tell me you're mine, beautiful Lauren."

Can I commit to being his? Do I want to be treated as his sex toy? Will this be all it is between us: sex? I'm okay with that, for now. "I'm yours, Mr. Grant."

The pressure from the head of his thick cock brushes up and down between my labia before he unhurriedly sinks into me, allowing me to savour every thick, solid inch as it burrows deeper. His pelvis rests against my ass cheeks after three attempts, and my walls strain to accommodate his girth.

Our moans blend as his chest lowers to my bound arms. Two gentle kisses precede a quick nip to the nape of my neck.

Ouch!

Do it again!

"You're so fucking tight, Lauren." He pulls back and slowly eases fully inside me, holds still for a beat, and then rises to stand tall with his groin pressed firmly against my bottom.

One hand grips my rope bound arms and the other spans my lower back. "Are you ready, Lauren?"

I nod because words fail me.

"Be a good girl and take my cock, but if you scream, the panties go back in your mouth, and I'll spank your ass red hot. Do you understand?"

I've never been spanked as an adult. Why does the threat thrill me?

It's an inappropriate time for humor, but here I am giggling like a fucking school girl. I didn't know the level of warped fuckery I'd enjoy. Am I sexually repressed? Will this unorthodox man introduce me to more kinks I don't know I have?

The power in his thrusts bruises the front of my thighs as I'm repeatedly rammed against the edge of his desk. He impales me again and again until my pussy spasms around his shaft as another orgasm shreds through me. The battle to restrain my screams has my jaw clenched so tight my teeth may break.

Impossibly, he maintains his pace. His desperate, animalistic grunts are like catnip to my arousal and urge me toward yet another climax. I can't breathe and don't try to. Let death take me.

With one hand on the ropes around my forearms, the other fists my hair at the root and pulls me back into an arch.

"My beautiful Lauren." His lips brush my cheek. "I've waited for you. Now you're mine."

Masculine hedonistic grunts fill the room. Three more vicious thrusts rock my body before pleasure stills him. His breath holds as he floats through his euphoria; lost in his own peaceful demise.

My sensitive vaginal walls feel every pulse of his cock as semen dumps in waves into the condom. His pleasure is mine. A calm satisfaction greater than the physical fills me. By allowing him to bind me—to play on his kink until he lost himself so completely—is better than any orgasm any man has taken from me. Why is that?

His weight eases off my back after a full moment, and we both whimper as his shrinking cock slips free. His hand spans over my upper back to keep my face down on his desk. “Stay here.”

I don’t move as fabric rustles before the brush of shoes along the carpet fades to my right. Water runs from a tap before he returns and weaves a warm washcloth delicately and respectfully through my sensitive vaginal folds. He cherishes my vagina, like fine China.

The cloth rests on the desk beside my hip, as his hands gingerly unbind my arms. His fingertips appreciate each tender indent the rope leaves behind. As the final knot releases, my arms are gently lowered. I hadn’t realized until now how sore my muscles were from the position, how my resistance made it worse. I may bear bruises tomorrow, but I don’t care.

His guidance is gentle as he directs me to sit in his chair. The leather is cool against my thighs.

Kneeling before me, he supports each forearm as he caresses the rope impressions.

“Are you okay?” Flushed cheeks stress the ebony of his eyes.

“Yes.” I can’t suppress my wildly inappropriate laughter. “Sorry, but that was really—” My brows climb over my widening eyes as my lungs empty through puckered lips.

His palm cups my cheek as he returns my smile. "You're incredible. I've waited so long to have you and here you are."

That can't be true. We've shared a polite smile but never interacted until we were stuck in the elevator. Well, not stuck, as it turned out.

My eyes roll. "You don't have to flatter me, Mr. Grant. You've already had me."

He blinks slowly as his shoulders square. "Rest assured; I'll never lie to you."

I squint to better assess the honesty bleeding into the fine wrinkles around his eyes. "If you wanted me, why didn't you approach me before?"

His hand pats my bare thigh before he stands to collect my dress, and confesses, "You know what office gossip is like. The last thing I want is for your reputation to be ground through the rumour mill. I hear it's vicious down there."

He's right; the watercooler crew would twitch with delight to start a new rumour about me trying to sleep my way to the top. Lucinda would literally vibrate as she hopped from one cubicle to the next, eager to spill while making each person promise not to tell anyone else.

At his beckoning, my arms rise over my head to allow him to slide the dress into place and zip the back. My bare ass is still on his leather chair. I probably won't get my panties back. Again.

"Thank you for being concerned for my reputation, but you could've sent a message for me to come to your office, or—"

A childlike excitement flitters through Mr. Grant's face. "I bided my time until an opportunity presented itself. The wait made the reward so much sweeter."

My head jerks left as my spine straightens. "The reward? I'm the reward? Really? Okay." My eyes roll, and he leans down to kiss my forehead.

"You are so much more than a reward." He pats my head like a dog before he collects a large brown paper bag from a side table. He sits on the chair opposite the desk from me and offers me a cardboard meal box from the bag. I'm given plastic utensils, a napkin, and a bottle of water, which he cracks open for me.

Freeing his utensils from the plastic bag, he says, "Lauren, tell me you want more, and I'll show you pleasure you've never dreamed of." He points his fork toward me. "You enjoyed being bound and taken. I want to explore that with you. Tell me you'll take this journey with me, or tell me to stop."

My fork stabs at the rice noodles and swirls. "Why do you always say, *Tell me to stop*? If you don't want to stop, why ask me to say it?"

Mr. Grant shrugs and copies my noodle play. "I don't want you to do anything you don't want to do, so it's my way of confirming you want to continue."

I look at him from below my brows and speak through a crooked grin. “Well, it’s sexy as fuck.”

He drinks me in with a ravenous gaze. “You’re sexy as fuck.”

“You’re insatiable, and because of that”—I lift the noodles to my lips and feign innocence—“I’ll sign your little contract.”

The wad of noodles enters my gaping mouth as his Adam’s apple bobs. “Lauren, you have no idea how pleased that makes me. In fact, I’ll prove it to you tomorrow evening when you come to my house to scene in my dungeon.”

My fork stills as a thrill of fear rushes my body. Hundreds of kinky scenarios suddenly crowd my mind.

“Dungeon?!”

~ The End ~

We hope you enjoyed reading “Tell Me to Stop.” May I ask you for a favour? Please take a moment to leave a review for this book. Each review helps bump this book into the search results for readers seeking books just like this one. By helping me, you’ll be helping them, too.

Thank you so much!

https://books2read.com/TellMeToStop

Goodreads

https://www.goodreads.com/book/show/248969852-tell-me-to-stop

Bookbub

https://www.bookbub.com/books/tell-me-to-stop-by-pebbles-lacasse

BONUS: Flip the page to read a sample of

COACHING RAYNA

BOOK ONE

Second Edition

Second Edition
COACHING
RAYNA
by Pebbles Lacasse

A case of opposites attract,
or fatal attraction?

He's ten years her junior, a bad boy bodybuilder, too wild to be tamed. He knows she deserves more than the likes of him. Nonetheless, she is the object of his fascination.

She's a divorced mother craving seduction by her brawny neighbour. She's lonely but has too much baggage to consider acting on her infatuation. He's worthy of an uninhibited, younger woman with a supreme body and a fierce sexual drive, none of which describes her.

One steamy summer afternoon has them unable to deny their needs. While Coach enlightens her about his savage sexual nature, Rayna teaches him that connecting on a deeper level can be more rewarding than anything he's experienced.

But not everyone is thrilled these opposites connected. As Rayna and Coach struggle to overcome the ghosts of their pasts together, toxic exes and psychopathic admirers refuse to be pushed aside, ruthlessly taking their revenge with a pound of flesh.

Can the two survive what they'll be forced to endure, or will their attraction end in disaster?

CHAPTER ONE

DOING the laundry isn't what I planned to do on my first Saturday off work in three weeks. Having lunch with my friends or taking the kids on an adventure would be so much more fun. But the chores have to get done. The kids are running out of clean clothes and all of my work scrubs are too dirty to wear again.

Shutting the door to the laundry room and pretending the piles of dirty clothes don't exist would be so much easier, but I can no longer avoid this mundane chore.

Would it kill the kids to throw in a load once in a while? I've taught them both how to do it, so I know their laziness isn't due to their lack of know-how. I'm a firm believer in teaching children how to do real-life tasks.

Instead of having a fun day with me, they're shut away in their rooms. To be honest, I'd rather that than have them follow me from room to room complaining that they're bored. Not like that's possible; their rooms are full of interesting distractions that should keep their imaginations alive and blooming.

I'm shaken from my thoughts. Is that a lawnmower I hear?

I immediately stop sorting colours from whites and pull the button to halt the gushing water filling the washing machine. I can't tell whether it's the dreamboat next door mowing his lawn or the neighbour directly behind my house...

My legs can't carry me up the stairs quick enough, even though I'm stepping two at a time. I nearly smack my head off the patio doors trying to look for him.

Yes! Damn, he's so fucking hot! I've been looking forward to this show all week.

I quickly pour a glass of wine three-quarters full of the nice pinot I opened last night. I must act aloof, as though I'm not outside to watch his sweaty, tanned skin as it stretches over his bloated muscles. My pussy tightens as I slide open the glass door and take a deep breath. Without glancing his way, I step out and close it behind me.

After setting my glass on the table, I squat my ass on the cushiony deckchair and rest my feet on the chair opposite. Being the smart cookie that I am, I always keep a book at the backdoor to make him think I'm reading and not ogling him while dreaming up a naughty fantasy.

Damn, it's hot today! I don't mind; the glistening sweat accentuates the ripples of muscle.

I always sit facing his yard. This way, I can drink him in without being too obvious. I open the book and pretend to read with my head tipped downward.

Nearly every Saturday for the past three years, I've lost myself in my imagination while staring at my hunky neighbour. His muscles flex as he pushes the mower around his enormous yard while wearing nothing but shoes and a pair of shorts that fit snug on his thick, muscular thighs.

His name is Simon Brenton, but everyone calls him Coach because he owns a gym and coaches people on how to reach their peak level of physical fitness. He's as strong as an ox; I can't stress that enough. The man's arms, chest, and thighs are massive, his waist tight and ripped. I imagine he can fuck like a machine.

The power behind those thunderous thighs would have any woman screaming through multiple orgasms until she lost consciousness.

My fantasies have me in his arms, his thin lips on mine, pelvis rhythmically grinding against my needy vagina as he sinks himself deep into me.

Sigh…

I'm divorced, thankfully. I've had no intimate encounters in the four years since I gave the asshole the boot. My life is too busy working and raising my kids. I'm sure that's why I love to picture myself getting sexually mauled by my hot neighbour more often than what's probably healthy for anyone.

The best thing that happened out of the shitty marriage is two children. Kim is eleven, and Ken is thirteen. There's never enough time in a day for us to connect other than dinner time when we sit at the table together and discuss what's on their minds. There are days when I almost have to poke them with a stick to get them to talk.

My son is getting to the age where he thinks mom isn't cool enough to hang out with anymore. He used to be my little shadow, clung to me wherever I'd go, but things have changed. I miss that. My daughter still enjoys my company, but I'm sure she'll think I'm stupid soon enough, especially if she takes after me. I was rude to my mother too often during my teen years. Hopefully, she'll be wiser than I was.

Between my job, the kids, and the household, I'm exhausted when I flop into bed at night. Doing everything myself, without a partner or an accountable ex, is sometimes overwhelming.

Sex comprises me occasionally masturbating while using my helpful aides: my fat dildo and a vibrator. I'm usually so tired at the end of the day that I only want to sleep. Sometimes, when I've been unusually excited—like after watching Coach mow his lawn, for instance—I'll zip through masturbation just to ease my sexual tension enough that I can sleep.

I've gone weeks without having an orgasm. It's depressing, I know. I used to be extremely sexually expressive. What happened to me?

Coach probably knows exactly why I'm out here, but he's kind enough not to call me out. If he looks up and sees me, he'll wave. I'll lift my head and wave back, and he'll continue to mow while I quietly observe his sculpted body. I'm sure he gets an ego boost from women checking him out, and I imagine it happens a lot. I'm an out of shape older woman and not his type.

Sometimes we chat over the fence, but it's rare. We've had conversations over the years, ranging from politics to religion and even about our childhoods.

He's intelligent and well-spoken, which I find to be an alluring trait in a man. The sexiest thing about him is his ability to hold eye contact and not flinch, which intimidates the hell out of me. He's definitely an assertive man, and that excites me. He's far more alluring than my arrogant, cheating coward of an ex-husband who has no spine to speak of.

Coach occasionally has his friends from the gym over to his place. I love those days! They're all fit and muscular like he is. They sit outside shirtless under the heat of the sun, and I can't stop watching their brawny chests and backs as they carry on, boasting about their wild adventures with naughty women, or telling tales of their high school football highlights.

I wonder what it would feel like to have one of their thick bodies above me, using those powerful thighs and strong backs to fuck me hard. My pussy twinges at the thought. I couldn't pick their faces out in a line-up even if I had to, because I never stop staring at their bodies. I wish I could see what they have in their shorts that might please me.

The day after Coach moved in, three years ago, I went over to introduce myself and welcome him to the neighbourhood. I was captivated by his physical size, but his confidence attracted me most. I could barely speak. Everything I muttered sounded stupid, especially when I asked to meet his wife and kids.

There was a woman and a few children helping with the move, so I assumed they were his family. That's when he told me that he's never married and never plans to. The woman was his sister, and they were her children. Strangely, it pleased me to know that he was available but sad that my excuse to visit with him for arranged playdates with our kids was now void.

Coach has had many women come and go, but his present girlfriend doesn't talk to me even if we're both outside. Occasionally she'll wave, but we've never carried on a conversation. She doesn't seem shy. Judging by the occasional leers directed at me, she dislikes me. I don't recall saying or doing anything to her she could have taken offensively.

I'd rather not get to know her well, anyway. It would be too hard to fantasize about her bulked-up man tearing off my clothes and ravishing me if she complains about all his nasty habits. That might turn me off, and then I'd be right back to having nothing tantalizing to stare at on these scorching summer days. This is all I have to make me feel like a sexual woman, and I need it. I don't want to see him as an actual person with flaws. He's the perfect sex machine—at least, in my vivid imagination.

My tummy flutters just before he bends to pick up the metal table to move it out of his way, allowing him easier access to mow the grass beneath. When he lifts, his muscles flex and his skin strains to maintain them, but he moves the heavy table with barely a struggle.

That task would take the effort of my ex-husband plus his clone if he had one. Thankfully, there aren't two of that asshole. Just one of him is too many.

I've sucked back the entire glass of wine way too quickly and it's already going to my head. Maybe I should have eaten something today before I bled this glass dry.

Coach finishes and puts the table back and the mower in the shed before starting to pick weeds out of his vegetable garden. I've never seen his girlfriend lift a finger to maintain the yard, even if a weed stands tall right beside her foot. I see the way he looks at her, and I don't think she'll be around much longer.

He's down on his widely spread knees and bent over to reach for a well-rooted weed. He pulls, flexing his back muscles ever so slightly. The lumps on his arm shift and grow as he moves, stirring something primal inside of me. His flesh glistens under the vibrant sun.

I want to taste him. I imagine what it must feel like to lie beneath such a powerful man, my legs wrapped around him while he looks down at me, readying himself to penetrate my body with his swollen manhood.

My eyes close and I take in a deep breath, suddenly realizing that my book rests on my lap, covering my hand slid down between my thighs. I've been pressing on my excited clit.

I jolt back to reality, yanking my hand from my groin. My eyes shift here and there, looking to see if anyone has been watching me masturbate through my shorts while I stare at the sexy guy next door like the neighbourhood pervert. I'm relieved no one else is outside until my eyes meet Coach's accusing glare.

He's still on his knees, but the table has turned, so to speak. He's been watching me. I want to run away and hide, but it's too late. There's no denying he saw what I was doing. I'm so embarrassed and the heat flushing through my cheeks proves it.

A smile slowly grows on his face. I try to return the gesture, but my bottom lip quivers, distorting my mouth. He probably can't see that detail from this distance. I feel the embarrassment continuing to fill my cheeks, proving my desire for him.

He lifts his thick arm to wave at me. I tip my head down while I wave, wishing I could go back in time to redo the last ten minutes. This time, I wouldn't have lost myself in the fantasy.

Coach tosses the weed he pulled before standing and brushing the dirt off his hands and knees. He looks up at me, still grinning like a man who has naughty intentions.

Oh shit! He's walking toward the fence separating our yards.

Should I go to the fence or tell him that I can't chat and then hide in the house? Damn it! I'm horribly embarrassed, but it would be rude to run away at this point. I grip the railing, fearing my trembling knees might give out, thus tumbling down the stairs in a most humiliating fashion. The way my luck is, it wouldn't surprise me.

As I approach the fence, his deep voice greets me. "Hi. Are you enjoying the day?"

The grin on his face boasts his sinful thoughts. His lips are thin, but the well-groomed beard and mustache frame them perfectly, as if they're a target for my lips to aim toward.

Snap out of it, damn it!

"Um, hi, Coach. It is a beautiful day." I swallow hard. "I see you mowed your lawn."

I sound like such an idiot. I'd have to be blind and deaf to not know he mowed it. Couldn't I have thought of something less ridiculous to say? Why can't I say anything brilliant to this man? I bite my lip again; I do that when I'm nervous or intimidated. At the moment, I'm both.

"So it would seem. You watched me mow my lawn." He accentuates the word "watched."

I can imagine what he wanted to say: "...while you were flicking your bean."

I'm so relieved that he's respectful enough not to comment on my masturbation, further humiliating me. I'm not even sure that's possible at this point.

I shrug, crossing my arms over my chest and trying to be aloof by looking anywhere other than at his seductive eyes. Even still, I feel their gaze burning into me. They stare right through me and into my soul, setting it on fire.

Fuck! Timidly, yet trying to seem nonchalant, I say, "Yeah, sorry. There's nothing else to look at that's remotely as exciting as you mowing your lawn."

Shit! I said he was exciting. Damn it!

"Watching me excites you?" He beams, resting his large, tattooed arms on the top of the slatted wood fence.

Each time we've talked in the past, he's been an absolute gentleman. He's insinuated nothing sexual could happen between us. Is it his intention to aim this conversation in that direction, or am I reading too much into his words?

"I don't know how to answer that. I mean, yes, you are nice to look at, obviously, and nobody else is outside, so there really is nothing…"

My words fall away. I swallow hard, suddenly realizing that my mouth is parched. I just might cough up the wad of cotton manifesting in my throat.

He must think I'm a sex-deprived, slightly older woman with ridiculous fantasies of being with a very fit younger man who has absolutely no reason to think of her as anything but a mother. He must laugh inside his head at my idiocy, but I'm relieved that he isn't blatantly obvious about it.

I'm not a perfectly thin or physically fit woman, but I'm not overweight. My stomach is still flat after having had two cesarean sections. I'm very proud of that. My legs are thick and strong, and my waist is small, but my butt is jigglier than I'd like and my arms are getting flabby. The best part of me is my breasts; they're large and still somewhat rest at the same altitude they originally grew at. Gravity hasn't had its demonic way with them yet, but I have noticed that they are not as solid as they were ten years ago.

I look up at him only to see his eyes staring at my breasts, which are barely hidden beneath my light pink halter top. I look down and discover my nipples have betrayed me. They're pointing straight out, directly at Coach, as if trying to torpedo me toward him.

He sighs and whispers, "You have beautiful breasts. I'd like to see them without the shirt."

Wait! What?

Shivers ripple up my spine, prickling my skin and forming tiny bumps from head to toe. Every strand of hair on my head feels like it's lifting. My bottom jaw once again quivers uncontrollably, so I bite my lip between my teeth but cannot hold it steady. I stare at his eyes a little too long and it feels very uncomfortable between us.

Say something!

“Thank you,” I whisper with barely an audible voice. Damn it, that was a dumb thing to say! I could have said something more flirtatious than that, such as, “I would like that, too.”

My eyes follow his Adam’s apple as it slowly bobs in his throat when he swallows. I would love to wrap my lips around it while he fucks me deeply. I shake my head, hoping to clear the arousing thought, but it lingers.

“In fact, I’d like to see your entire nude body. You’re a sexy woman. You know that, right?”

“Um...” I stutter, “I-I am?” Oh please, compliment me again.

He chuckles, replying, “Sweet thing, I know you watch me, but what you don’t know is that I watch you, too. I can see straight into your kitchen from my office window.”

He turns to point to the window facing my house. My eyes look back at his in time to see his tongue lick his top lip.

He confesses, “I positioned my desk so I can catch glances of you while I work. When you’re in the kitchen at night, in that light blue nightgown, the really thin one," he pauses, "Well, it's my favourite. With the light behind you, I can see the silhouette of your amazing body. I fantasize about touching you over that nightgown."

My eyes are wide, face flushed a feverish red, and my mouth hangs open in surprise.

"Do you have any idea how often I jerk off while watching you make your kids' lunches at night?" he pauses again. "Almost every night."

Oh my God! Did I just hear that? He finds me sexy and masturbates while watching me perform a mundane task. Holy shit! No, he must be taunting me simply to see my reaction and then he'll let me down hard. A guy like him doesn't fantasize about a mother of two who's ten years older than him. He can have almost any young, fit woman he desires.

"You do?" I ask doubtfully. My mouth is painfully dry, and that glass of wine I guzzled is making me feel more uninhibited than my usual self. "I like watching you. I touch myself sometimes."

His sexy crooked smile is enough to make me swoon, but when his eyebrows bounce only once, my knees weaken. He radiates testosterone like an invisible aphrodisiac, making my thoughts cloudy. My pussy is so wet that I can feel its slickness. I wonder if other women experience his allure as intensely as I do. How could they not? He sure knows how to turn up the heat.

“Do you want to come over for another glass of wine?” he suggests with a deeper than usual voice.

He’s sporting a very serious expression with salacious eyes that seem to pierce right through me. I can’t prevent them from reading my deepest, darkest thoughts.

A bead of sweat trickles down the tanned skin on his well-formed bicep, and I nearly lean in to lick it simply to quench my ravenous thirst. My curiosity and desires are no longer my kept secret. I’ve opened a can of worms here, but I’m not sure I want to put the lid back on it yet. I’ve fantasized about this moment so many times.

In those dreams, he’s always lived up to my expectations. What if he doesn’t compare in reality? The fantasy will forever be tainted.

But what if he does?

“Yes, but I shouldn’t,” I reply, hating myself for turning down his offer. Whether or not his performance measures up to my high expectations,

I'm sure we could have had an entire afternoon of steamy sex, had I accepted the offer, but I have priorities. "The kids are home and they'd eventually notice my absence."

He suggests, "Tell them you're going for a walk. I won't keep you more than an hour…unless you'd like me to. I'll gladly entertain you for the rest of the day."

I swallow hard while forcing myself to look anywhere but at his beckoning brown eyes. My body trembles and my skin craves his touch. His gigantic hands would feel so rough against my womanly flesh. Having two of his fingers inside of me, pleasuring me while he kisses and suckles my nipples, would drive me to cum within seconds.

My legs wobble, weak from the thought. I quickly grab the fence to steady myself. Surely, he knows the effect he's having on me.

His hand hovers over mine, middle finger delicately caressing my middle digit. The contact feels electric. A whimper escapes me. My eyes meet his once again. A smirk has grown on his thin lips and his eyes seem darker, so much more dangerous and enticing than I've ever witnessed. I'd be a fool to deny myself this opportunity. It'll likely never happen again.

"Okay, but I need a little time."

I have done no maintenance on myself for a very long time. Sex is absent from my life, so I don't bother. My stomach tightens like a vice when he wraps his massive hand around my wrist, slowly and assertively pulling me closer to the fence. We are face to face, looking at one another, our breath brushing over each other's faces. My entire body shakes, and I can't control it.

"Don't take too long, okay?" he whispers. His sweet breath is hotter than the summer breeze that caused his skin to glisten so perfectly. "When you're ready, walk in the front door and come down the stairs. I'll be waiting for you."

He releases my wrist but watches me as I slowly ascend the stairs, painfully aware that my weak legs could fail me at some point. I can feel the heat from his stare as it burns into my body.

The instant I'm inside the house and sure he can't see me, I slide down the wall, planting my ass on the cool hardwood floor. I rub my wrist, making sure he isn't still attached to me. My skin is super-heated from just one touch.

How will his touch to my more delicate regions affect me?

My endorphins are easing; panic sets in. Oh god, what have I done? I can't go to his place! If I walk into that house and he touches me, I know I won't be able to maintain control over my primal needs.

Do I want to hold back though? That's a good question. It's been too long since anyone has touched me. I hope I don't make a fool of myself.

Shit!

Even though I'm still unsure if I'm going to go see him, I hop in the shower and shave away all my stubble. I wash my hair and my skin with the prettiest scented products I own.

Yes, I think I'm going over there.

No, no, I can't!

But I really, really want to. I deserve this, don't I?

After quickly drying my hair and dusting some powder on my face to reduce the shine, I flip through my closet, looking for something to wear that might be appropriate, but everything I own is so damn boring. I've been a single, overworked mom for so long that my sexy attire has been stowed in boxes or given away. I figured someone should get use out of them.

Frustrated, I settle for a light summer dress and a pair of white silky panties.

I'm still shaking when I enter my daughter's doorway. She's sitting on her bed reading a book assigned to her for a school project. Knowing her as I do, I'm sure it's due soon. She puts everything off to the last minute. She's always looking for an excuse to avoid anything that doesn't completely captivate her attention.

"Hi, baby. I'm going for a walk."

"Can I come?" she asks while bookmarking her page and edging herself off the bed.

"No, you have to get that book read. When is the project due?"

"In two days," she confesses, pouting.

I sigh heavily and give her the GET IT DONE look. "Okay then, you'd better get busy reading. I'll be back in about an hour."

"That's a long walk. Where are you going?" she asks with her face crinkled up as she re-situates herself on her bed.

"Just walking. I need some exercise and the fresh air will help me clear my thoughts." I try to sound convincing. "Don't worry, you won't even miss me."

I blow her a kiss only to witness the infamous eye roll. She acts like she's too mature for silly love gestures.

I enter my son's doorway, even more nervous now. I take a deep breath to calm myself before poking my head in. "Hey, I'm going for a walk. You don't want to come with, do you?"

He turns his contorted face to ensure I see the over-exaggerated expression of his disinterest.

"Okay then, keep an eye on your sister and don't go anywhere."

Without a word, he turns back to his computer to continue with his online game. Maybe they won't miss me.

I make my way out of my house, locking the door behind me. …

Did you enjoy the first chapter of COACHING RAYNA? It's a two-book series with excellent reviews. You can read this entire series by scanning the QR Code below or typing in one of the links into any search engine.

Book One:

Universal Link:
https://books2read.com/CoachingRayna-BookOne
Amazon.com
https://www.amazon.com/dp/B08KDWHB6Q

Or get both books together at a discount:

Universal Link:
https://books2read.com/TheCoachingRaynaSeries
Amazon.com
https://www.amazon.com/dp/B0BRGKGKNP

YOU MAY ALSO ENJOY:

First Chapter Teasers of 14 Books

TEASE

Full Novel Series

The Complete My JoeSmith Collection or buy individual books:
My JoeSmith: Anonymity, Book One
My JoeSmith: Anonymity, Book Two
My JoeSmith: Nurture, Book Three
My JoeSmith: Unity, Book Four

The Coaching Rayna Boxed Set or buy individual books:
Coaching Rayna, Book One
Coaching Rayna: Bound Hearts, Book Two

The Naughty Goldie Series or buy individual books:
Goldilocks & The Three Bear Brothers, Book One
Goldilocks & The Three Bear Brothers: Trifecta, Book Two
Goldilocks & The Three Bear Brothers: Overture, Book Three
Goldilocks & The Three Bear Brothers: Liberated, Book Four

Rule Breakers Standalone Series
My Best Friend's Brother
The Widowed
The Rockstar's Bodyguard

Full Novel Standalones

My Wife and Master Jake
Broken Charm
Snowman's Burden

Short Stories

Little Miss Muffet
Hello, Officer
Mistress Rabbit
A Run with Charley
Carter's Mistress
A Dominant's Favour

Still Waters Burn Deep
Dominatrix for Hire
Tell Me to Stop

Anthologies

Quarantined: A Boxed Set of Pandemic Proportions
Ignited by Hope 2025
Stuck on You 2025

+++++

To read teasers and see book cover photoshoot photos by Pebbles,

visit https://www.PebblesLacasse.com

Scan for Ebook Catalogue

ABOUT THE AUTHOR

Pebbles is an Amazon top-selling romantic erotica author of plot-driven contemporary suspense.

She loves to make readers' hearts throb and entertain their minds while leaving their bodies tingling with desire. She leans toward spinning tales of bad boys with big hearts desiring women who didn't know they had a kinky side. However, she's also known for her stories of women with hardened shells and a dominant nature, but they hold a secret yearning to be loved.

Her books and short stories often take her readers into the BDSM lifestyle while revolving around real-life issues.

There's always a happy-ever-after or happy-for-now ending because we all want life to work out in the end. Her captivating stories of romance, love, and tender moments keep her readers coming back for the next hottest story.

As someone living with Porphyria, Pebbles stays indoors to avoid UV light. It's not all bad since this allows her plenty of time to write. That's not to say she doesn't love glamping, fishing, kayaking, and swimming; she simply does it with protective clothing. Where there's a will, there's a way!

Pebbles is very family-oriented. She and her husband of 30+ years raised their children in southern Ontario, where she was born and remains to this day.

CONNECT WITH PEBBLES

Scan to Discover All of Pebbles' Links Online:

SUBSCRIBE TO PEBBLES' NEWSLETTER

Sign up to receive Pebbles Lacasse's newsletter and receive a free short story to welcome you. Be among the first to read teasers from the books she's writing, learn what Pebbles does to keep her busy when she isn't writing her steamy novels, discover the captivating authors she's reading, be led to books with similar genres grouped together just for readers like you, and other crazy antics.

https://bit.ly/pebbleskinkynews

JOIN PEBBLES' TEAMS

Are you an **influencer** interested in Pebbles and her books? Would you like to be a valued member of Pebbles' ***ARC team*? Advanced Readers** receive copies of her soon-to-be published novels to read with the promise to leave reviews by the date set by Pebbles. *You'll get **her books for FREE** forever as long as you leave reviews!*

Sound like a good deal?

https://forms.gle/gseo39XRubENVWjA9
or scan using your camera

WHY DOES PEBBLES WRITE BDSM EROTIC ROMANCE?

Erotica captivates me and for this reason I write it. It's not all about sex, much like real life. It's the romance, love and tender touches that keep us coming back for more. We all want to be loved, adored and cherished. BDSM gives us all of that and more. Yes, it can be cold and emotionless, but it doesn't have to be. My books show the pain and pleasure associated with the BDSM lifestyle, but they also show the unbreakable, loving commitment between the Dom and Sub. The trust built by this play is undeniable.

Thus, I love to write BDSM Erotic Romance.

Always, *Pebbles Lacasse*

https://linktr.ee/pebbleslacasse

www.ingramcontent.com/pod-product-compliance
Lightning Source LLC
LaVergne TN
LVHW010940110826
845149LV00013B/2695

* 9 7 8 1 9 8 9 9 7 9 6 9 3 *